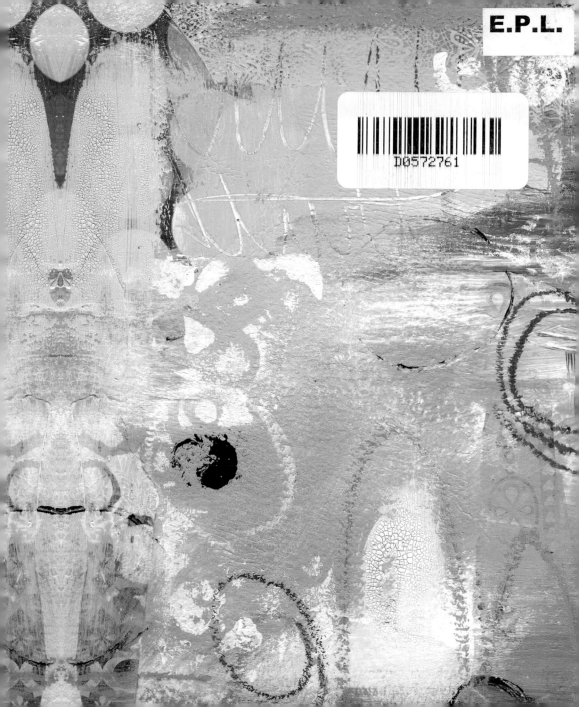

This book is dedicated to Owen.
You will always be my little deer.

It is also dedicated to the
thousands of Métis and
Aboriginal children who
grew up never knowing their
totem animal.

SOMETIMES
I FEEL
LIKE A FOX

Danielle Daniel

Groundwood Books
House of Anansi Press
Toronto Berkeley

Sometimes I feel like a bear,
strong and confident.
I stand tall and growl
and protect those around me.

Sometimes I feel like a deer,
sensitive and kind.
I listen to the sounds in the distance
and prance throughout the forest.

Sometimes I feel like a beaver,
busy and purposeful.
I only use what I need
and always get the job done.

Sometimes I feel like a butterfly,
delicate and free.
I spread my wings wide open
and flutter from flower to leaf.

Sometimes I feel like a moose,
awkward yet graceful.
I move swiftly and silently,
with a gentle strength and wisdom.

Sometimes I feel like an owl,
intuitive and discreet.
I fly across the dark night sky,
always watching and listening.

Sometimes I feel like a rabbit,
quick and alert.
I like to eat my carrots
and leap into new adventures.

Sometimes I feel like a turtle,
slow and quiet.
I retreat into my shell
and find peace and solitude.

Sometimes I feel like a wolf,
intelligent and loyal.
I surround myself with family
and howl into the moonlight.

Sometimes I feel like a porcupine,
innocent and curious.
I have a big imagination
and know how to protect myself.

Sometimes I feel like a raven,
dark and mysterious.
I am both messenger and secret keeper
and help bring light from darkness.

Sometimes I feel like a fox,
sly and sharp.
I observe all those around me
and disappear quickly.

Totem Animals and Their Meanings

Bear	brave
Deer	loving
Beaver	determined
Butterfly	vulnerable
Moose	strong
Owl	wise
Rabbit	creative
Turtle	patient
Wolf	loyal
Porcupine	curious
Raven	truthful
Fox	clever

Author's Note

The word *totem*, or *doodem* in Anishinaabe, means clan. In the Anishinaabe tradition, everyone belongs to an animal clan, which is decided at birth and is usually the same as their father's. This totem animal symbolizes the skills that each member of the clan must learn to serve their tribe. People from the same *doodem* are considered brothers and sisters and cannot marry, but they have a collective duty to care for one another. Animal totems continue to be an important part of being Anishinaabe.

Animal totems are also known as animal guides. In my book, a selection of totems act as guides to help children identify with the positive character traits of animals that may be familiar to them. Although children may associate with different animal guides throughout their lives, it is commonly believed that one animal acts as their main guide. This connection can be shared through physical interaction, dreams, mutual characteristics or personal interest. The animal instructs and protects the child as they experience their physical and spiritual life.

Totem animals remind us that all living organisms are part of the same cycle of life.

Groundwood Books / House of Anansi Press
groundwoodbooks.com

We acknowledge for their financial support of our publishing program the Canada
Council for the Arts, the Ontario Arts Council and the Government of Canada.

 Canada Council   Conseil des Arts
for the Arts   du Canada

 ONTARIO ARTS COUNCIL
CONSEIL DES ARTS DE L'ONTARIO
an Ontario government agency
un organisme du gouvernement de l'Ontario

With the participation of the Government of Canada | Canadä
Avec la participation du gouvernement du Canada

Library and Archives Canada Cataloguing in Publication
Daniel, Danielle, author, illustrator
Sometimes I feel like a fox / written and illustrated by Danielle Daniel.
Poems.
Issued in print and electronic formats.
ISBN 978-1-55498-750-4 (bound).—ISBN 978-1-55498-751-1 (pdf)
1. Totems—Juvenile poetry. 2. Animals—Juvenile poetry. I. Title.
PS8607.A55645S66 2015   jC811'.6   C2015-900034-3
C2015-90003

The illustrations were done in acrylic on canvas.
Design by Michael Solomon
Printed and bound in Canada

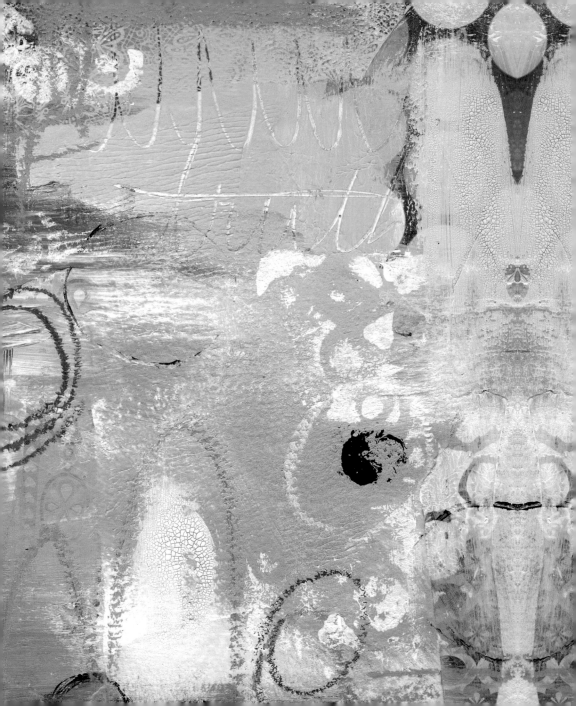